This book belongs to:

_____

Disney
Tuck-in Tales

Stories About Kindness

DISNEY
Tuck-in Tales

Stories About Kindness

SCHOLASTIC INC.

New York   Toronto   London   Auckland   Sydney
Mexico City   New Delhi   Hong Kong   Buenos Aires

Published by Scholastic Inc.,
90 Old Sherman Turnpike, Danbury, Connecticut 06816.

ISBN 0-545-00298-2

Printed in the U.S.A.
First printing, May 2007

Story illustrations by Alvin S. White Studio
Designed by North Woods Design Group

CONTENTS

Disney·PIXAR
MONSTERS, INC.

Scared Silly

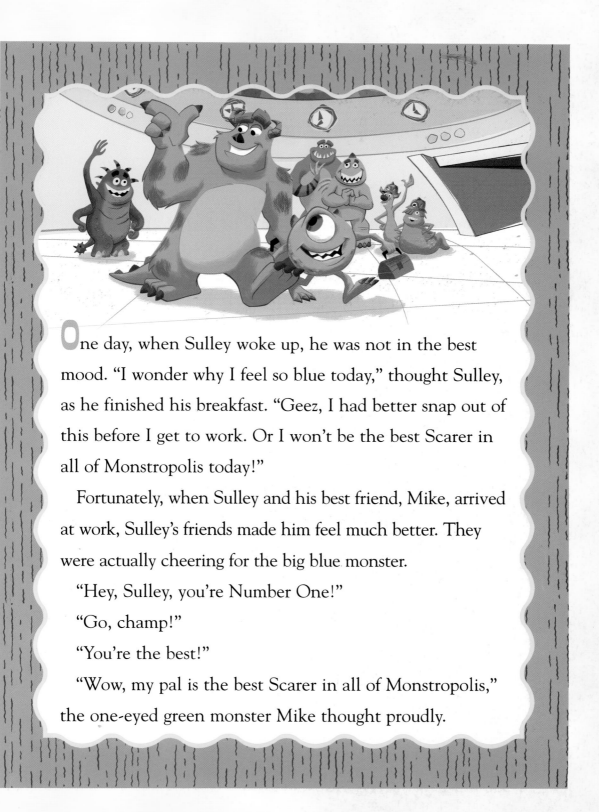

One day, when Sulley woke up, he was not in the best mood. "I wonder why I feel so blue today," thought Sulley, as he finished his breakfast. "Geez, I had better snap out of this before I get to work. Or I won't be the best Scarer in all of Monstropolis today!"

Fortunately, when Sulley and his best friend, Mike, arrived at work, Sulley's friends made him feel much better. They were actually cheering for the big blue monster.

"Hey, Sulley, you're Number One!"

"Go, champ!"

"You're the best!"

"Wow, my pal is the best Scarer in all of Monstropolis," the one-eyed green monster Mike thought proudly.

While Sulley did his warm-up scare exercises, Mike brought out a door to a child's room. Then he put a scream canister in place and waited for the light to flash. As soon as the light signaled, Sulley ran through the door into a child's room.

"*Grrr!*" Sulley growled, as the door was closing.

"*AAAAAAAAH!*" Mike heard a kid scream.

"Wow, listen to that!" said Mike.

Later that night, Mike told his girlfriend, Celia, "I wonder sometimes what it would be like to be a top Scarer, like Sulley."

"Oh, Schmoopsie-poo, you're a *funny* monster," she said. "You couldn't scare a flea!"

Mike was determined, though. He would show her. He would show everyone that he could be scary, just like Sulley.

The next day, Mike carried a big bag to work.

"What's in the bag?" asked Sulley.

"I'm not telling," Mike answered.

"Oh," Sulley said quietly, a little bit hurt by Mike's attitude.

Mike waited until Sulley went through a door. Then he pulled a purple fright wig and two great big shoes with claws out of the bag.

"Boo!" Mike shouted when Sulley dashed back through the door.

"Aaah!" yelled Sulley. Thud! He tripped over Mike's shoes. "What did you do that for?" Sulley asked, rubbing the bump on his head.

"Did I scare you?" Mike asked.

"No, but you certainly surprised me!" Sulley replied.

"Oh," said a disappointed Mike. But he wasn't going to give up.

That night, Mike left work without Sulley. The big blue monster had to walk home alone. He wondered why Mike hadn't waited for him.

When Sulley arrived home, the apartment was dark.

"Mike, where are you?" called Sulley.

"*Wooooooooo!*" a strange voice wailed. Mike jumped out from behind the kitchen door. He was smeared with gooey red tomato sauce from head to toe. Slimy spaghetti trailed off his ears and dangled from his fingers.

"I'm a noodle monster!" Mike screeched.

Sulley started to laugh. He laughed so hard that he had to lie down.

Mike stared at his friend. "I suppose that means you weren't scared," he said finally.

Sulley was gasping from laughing so hard. "No, but you are very funny!"

Mike stomped into his bedroom and closed the door. Sulley stood outside.

"Come on, Mike. Open up!" Sulley called, knocking on the door.

"Go away," a very unhappy Mike answered.

That night, Sulley had to eat dinner and watch TV without his best friend to keep him company. "This place just isn't the same without Mike," thought Sulley. "The food's no good, the TV's no good—nothing's good. . . ."

The next morning, when Sulley woke up, Mike had left. Sulley had to walk to work by himself. He felt lonely and sad. "Why is Mike acting so strangely? Is he angry about something?" Sulley wondered.

When Sulley got to work, he went to the locker room to get ready. But he didn't feel much like doing his job. He was too worried about the way Mike was behaving. "I wish I could make Mike feel better. But what can I do?" Sulley asked himself.

Just as Sulley opened his locker door—*bam!*—Mike jumped out. He was painted blue and covered with fur, just like Sulley. He was wearing stilts to make himself as tall as Sulley.

"Aw, Mike, what's wrong with you?" asked Sulley. "Why are you making fun of me? I thought you were my friend."

Sulley's feelings were really hurt this time. He hurried off to the Scare Floor.

Mike tried to catch up to Sulley. But the green-eyed monster was too clumsy on his stilts. "Stop! Come back, Sulley," Mike yelled. "Look at me! I'm scary like you!"

A bunch of the other monsters at Monsters, Inc. stopped what they were doing and began to follow Mike and Sulley.

"Ha-ha—what a joker!" one shouted.

"Mike, you're the funniest," another yelled.

"Stop, Mike—you're going to make me bust my fangs laughing," yet another monster called out.

"But I'm not funny, I'm scary!" Mike exclaimed. He took a huge breath. "Watch this!"

"*RRRRrrrrrrr!*" roared Mike.

"*EEEEeeeeeee!*" Mike shrieked, as his stilts flew out from under him.

"*Yow-ow-ow!*" groaned Mike, as he hit the floor, bounced, and rolled over and over.

"Ha, ha, ha!" the other monsters shouted with laughter.

Mike rolled to a stop beside Sulley's gigantic feet. He sat up with a moan and rubbed his head.

When Sulley saw his friend on the floor, he immediately stopped feeling sorry for himself and asked, "Mike, Mike, are you all right?" Then Sulley whispered to his best friend, "Mike, what is it you're trying to do? Maybe I can help you."

"I wanted to be scary—to see if I could scare someone," Mike quietly explained, as Sulley helped him to stand. "But I'm no good at it. And scaring is what's important around here." The little green monster's one eye drooped. "See, everyone's laughing—nobody's scared."

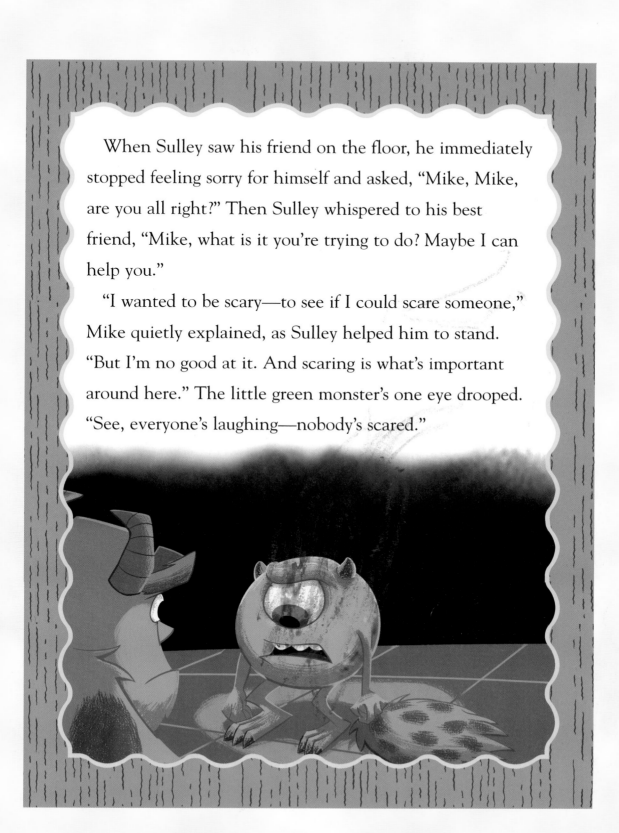

Sulley looked around. Mike was right—everyone was laughing. But that was because Mike was funny, and everyone liked him for it. Mike made people feel better by making them laugh.

"Look, Mike, that's what *everyone* likes about you—that you make them laugh," said Sulley. "You make people feel better when they laugh," he added. "Besides, you had *me* scared!"

"Oh, really—how?" Mike wondered.

"Well, it's like this, Mike," Sulley answered. "Not only did I think you were hurt, but I also thought you were going to stop being my best pal. And both are just about the scariest things I could ever imagine."

Mike gently punched his friend's arm. Together, they strolled down the hall.

"Stop being your best pal?" exclaimed Mike. "Aw, Sulley, don't make me laugh."

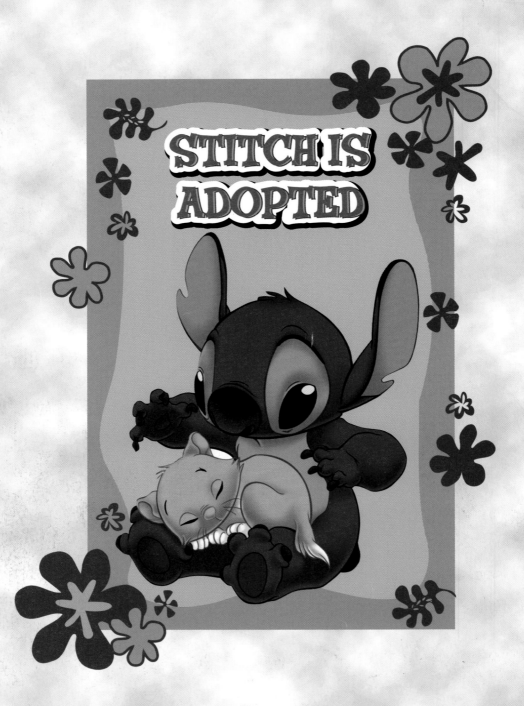

Stitch was waiting for Lilo to come home from school when she burst into the house, carrying a puppy.

"Hi, Stitch!" called Lilo. "My friend Leilani asked me to take care of her puppy, Rover, while she visits her grandmother."

"Stitch wants to listen to Elvis," Stitch said.

"Not now," Lilo answered. "I have to take good care of Rover."

Stitch watched Lilo feed Rover and make him a bed. Stitch watched her scratch Rover's ears and rub his tummy. Meanwhile, Lilo wasn't paying any attention to Stitch.

"Can we listen to Elvis now?" Stitch asked.

"I want to teach Rover some new tricks," said Lilo.

Stitch watched Lilo teach Rover to sit up and to lie down. She showed him how to roll over. She threw balls for the puppy and gave him treats.

That evening, Nani and Lilo watched Rover play
tug-of-war with the kitchen rug. "Oh, isn't he cute!"
exclaimed Nani. They laughed at everything Rover did.
They weren't paying any attention to Stitch.

Stitch went to bed feeling left out and sad. "Maybe if I act
like a puppy," he thought, "Lilo will pay attention to me."

The next morning, Stitch tried to act like Rover. He hid
Lilo's shoes and chewed the
kitchen rug. But that only
made Lilo angry.

"You need a time out,"
she told Stitch. "Go to
our room while I take
Rover for a walk."

Stitch waited until Lilo and Rover left. Then Stitch hurried outside and ran towards town.

When Lilo and Rover came home, it was time for her to go to her hula class. She searched all of Stitch's best hiding places. But Lilo couldn't find Stitch anywhere. She wondered why he wasn't home.

"Stitch loves dancing the hula," Lilo thought. "I guess I'll have to go without him."

Stitch wasn't home when Lilo returned from dance, either. "Have you seen Stitch?" she asked Nani and her friend David.

Before they could answer, Cobra Bubbles the social worker knocked at the door. "You need to hide Stitch," he told them. "Two scientists from the Department for the Study of Aliens are looking for him. They want to take him to their laboratory and study him."

"But I don't know where Stitch is!" exclaimed Lilo. "He's gone!"

"Well, I suggest you find him before the scientists do," Cobra replied.

Lilo and Nani hurried to town to look for Stitch. Meanwhile, Cobra and David drove to the beach to look for him, too.

"Stitch has been acting weird all day," Lilo told Nani, as they searched. "His badness level was way up. He hid my shoes and chewed the rug. He acted just like Rover!"

US MAIL

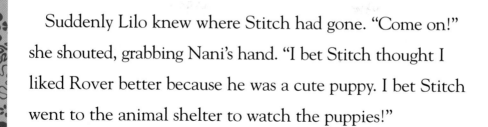

Suddenly Lilo knew where Stitch had gone. "Come on!" she shouted, grabbing Nani's hand. "I bet Stitch thought I liked Rover better because he was a cute puppy. I bet Stitch went to the animal shelter to watch the puppies!"

Sure enough, when they reached the shelter, Stitch was there closely watching two cute puppies.

"Stitch learning to be cute like puppy," Stitch explained when he saw Lilo. "So Lilo like him again."

"Oh, Stitch," cried Lilo, "I like you just the way you are. I'm sorry I didn't show it. Now let's go home!"

31

But when they started to leave, they saw the two scientists walking towards them.

"Nani!" Lilo said. "We have to do something!"

Nani found two dust mops with some cleaning supplies. She tied the dust mops onto Stitch so that he looked like a floppy-haired puppy.

Lilo put a leash on Stitch, and together, they walked slowly out of the shelter and past the scientists. The scientists watched Stitch suspiciously.

Just then Cobra Bubbles and David arrived at the animal shelter.

"Hey, scientists!" called David. "We just saw an alien heading out to sea. You had better hurry if you want to catch him. Hop in the car, and we'll take you there."

The scientists jumped into the car, and Cobra Bubbles and David sped away.

Nani, Lilo, and Stitch were finally safe!

As soon as they got home, Lilo and Nani made a pink-frosted cake with the word 'ohana written on top.

As they began to eat the cake, Cobra Bubbles and David came back.

"Well, we solved that problem," Cobra said. "The scientists are heading out to sea to look for Stitch," he added. "He's safe for now."

"And look what I found at the beach," said David. He lifted a kitten out of a bag and set it on the floor.

"I thought she needed a good home," David said.

"How cute!" Lilo said. Stitch watched quietly as everyone played with the kitten.

But before Stitch could start to feel sad and left out again, the kitten climbed onto his lap and fell asleep. Stitch felt warm and happy inside.

"Stitch never had a pet before," he said. "Can Stitch keep kitten, please?"

"Yes," Nani answered kindly. "In fact, I think that kitten has just adopted you as its family."

"And you know what that means," said Lilo.

Stitch nodded solemnly. "'*Ohana*—it means 'family.' In a family, we are kind to each other; and nobody—Stitch or kitten—gets left out!"

The Sticky Honey Pot

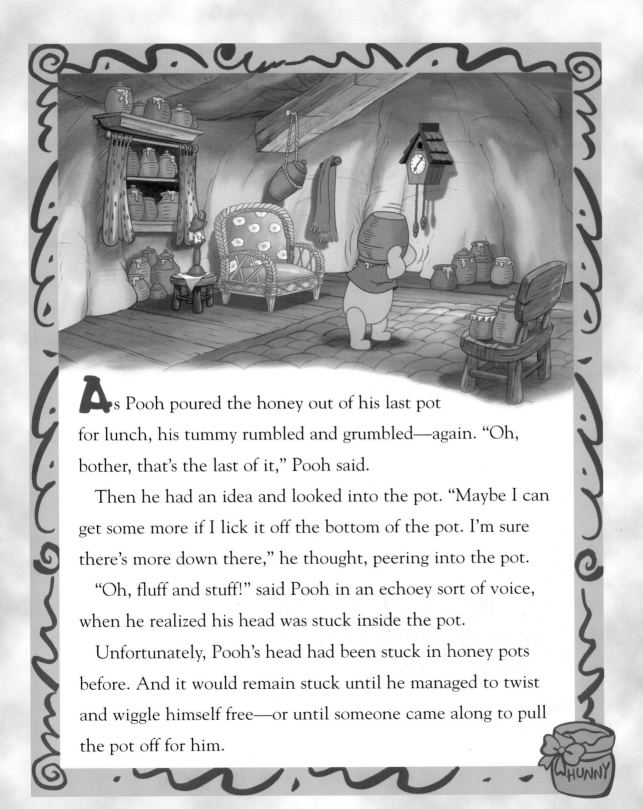

As Pooh poured the honey out of his last pot for lunch, his tummy rumbled and grumbled—again. "Oh, bother, that's the last of it," Pooh said.

Then he had an idea and looked into the pot. "Maybe I can get some more if I lick it off the bottom of the pot. I'm sure there's more down there," he thought, peering into the pot.

"Oh, fluff and stuff!" said Pooh in an echoey sort of voice, when he realized his head was stuck inside the pot.

Unfortunately, Pooh's head had been stuck in honey pots before. And it would remain stuck until he managed to twist and wiggle himself free—or until someone came along to pull the pot off for him.

On this particular occasion, Pooh was really in a lot of trouble. His head was wedged quite tightly, and there was no one around to help. So he decided to look for help. But having a pot on one's head makes looking for others somewhat difficult.

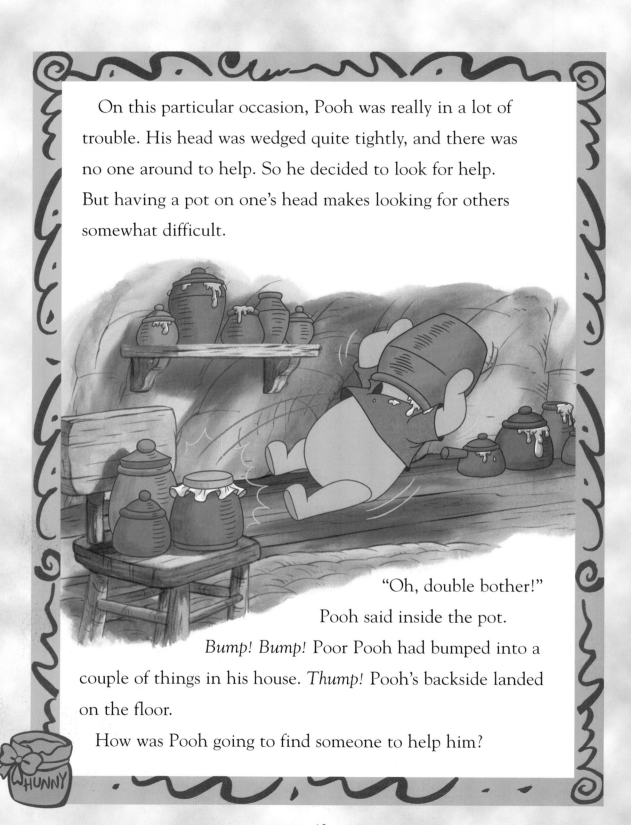

"Oh, double bother!"
Pooh said inside the pot.
Bump! Bump! Poor Pooh had bumped into a couple of things in his house. *Thump!* Pooh's backside landed on the floor.

How was Pooh going to find someone to help him?

Then he had an idea. This made Pooh rather proud, because bears of very little brain don't often have ideas.

"I shall find my way outside, where someone will find me!" Pooh decided.

Feeling very pleased with himself, Pooh managed to come up with a way (with a few more bumps and thumps) to move across the room to his open door.

"Lovely," Pooh said to himself (only it sounded more like *lumply* from inside the honey pot). "Now I shall simply wait for someone to come by and help me."

And so he did. Pooh waited and waited, and then he
waited some more. He tried humming to himself, but he
became confused by the echoes, so he stopped. Then Pooh
tried tapping his foot, but that didn't seem to be all that
interesting. At last, Pooh fell asleep.

After a bit, Pooh's good friend Piglet came by for a visit.
Piglet was puzzled when he saw his good friend sitting on a
tree stump outside his door with a honey pot on his head
and making a strange noise.

"Pooh?" Piglet asked tentatively.

"Mmmmmmmm-pffff. Mmmmmmmm-PFFFF," said Pooh.

"Oh, did I interrupt your lunch?" asked Piglet. "Perhaps I should come back later," he suggested.

"Um-hmmmm," Pooh snored. But Piglet thought Pooh had said *Uh-huh* as in *Yes, please do return later.*

Piglet left without Pooh even knowing his good friend had visited. "Good-bye, Pooh," Piglet said. "I'll come back later."

Soon after, Tigger arrived at Pooh's house.

"Hi ya, Pooh Bear!" Tigger said, bouncing atop Pooh.

"Oof! Oof!" said Pooh. But to Tigger, it sounded as if Pooh had said *Hoo-hoo!*

"That's right, Pooh Boy!" cried Tigger. "I say that, too. Only sometimes, I add an extra *Hoo!* to make it extra-specially tiggery. Hoo-hoo-HOO!"

Pooh didn't hear a thing Tigger was saying. He was simply trying to catch his breath after being bounced.

"Well," Tigger said, "I got some more bouncin' ta do. See ya later, Pooh Bear. Hoo-hoo-HOO!"

Tigger bounced Pooh one last time before he left, leading Pooh to say once again, "Oof!" This delighted Tigger, because he believed Pooh was talking to him.

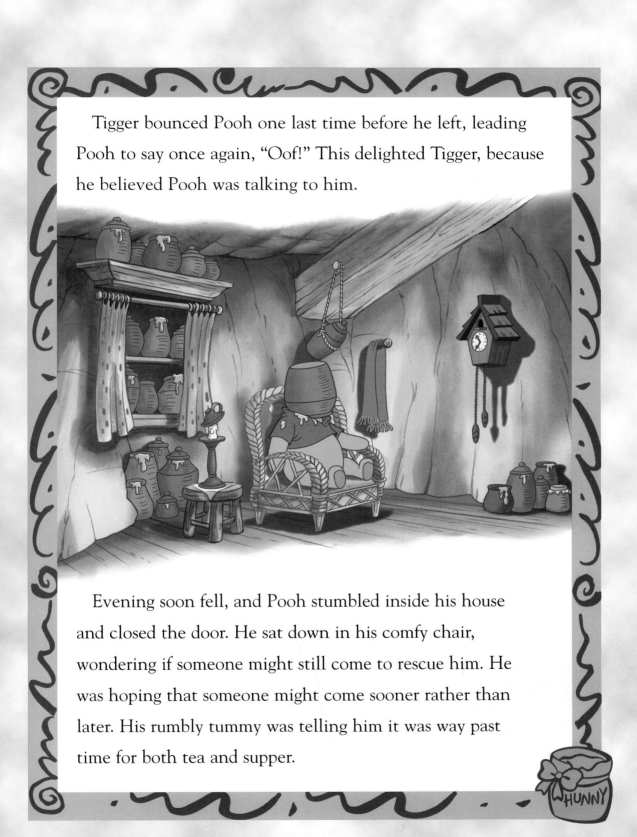

Evening soon fell, and Pooh stumbled inside his house and closed the door. He sat down in his comfy chair, wondering if someone might still come to rescue him. He was hoping that someone might come sooner rather than later. His rumbly tummy was telling him it was way past time for both tea and supper.

At last, someone tapped loudly at Pooh's door. But, of course, Pooh didn't hear it.

Christopher Robin popped his head inside and found his best bear sitting quietly in his comfy chair with a honey pot wedged tightly over his head.

"Oh, Pooh, you silly old bear!" said Christopher Robin playfully. "I've been looking everywhere for you. I haven't seen you all day, and I thought—"

Christopher Robin suddenly stopped talking. He realized that Pooh probably could not hear a word he was saying. So he went over to Pooh and tapped very gently on the honey pot.

Pooh sat up straight and shouted, "Come on in!" He thought someone was knocking at his door. But all Christopher Robin heard was, *Kooo-eeee!*

Christoher Robin had seen Pooh stuck in this type of situation before. Christopher twisted and turned the pot ever so gently trying to get it off Pooh's head.

But no matter which way Christopher Robin twisted, turned, and pulled at the honey pot, it simply would not budge.

Then Christopher Robin had an idea. He went over to Pooh's kitchen sink, found a cloth, and dipped it into some warm, soapy water. Gently, Christopher Robin wiped away the gooey honey that was sticking all around Pooh's head and neck.

After a while, Christopher Robin gave one last yank on the honey pot.

Pop!

Off came the pot, and out popped Pooh's head.

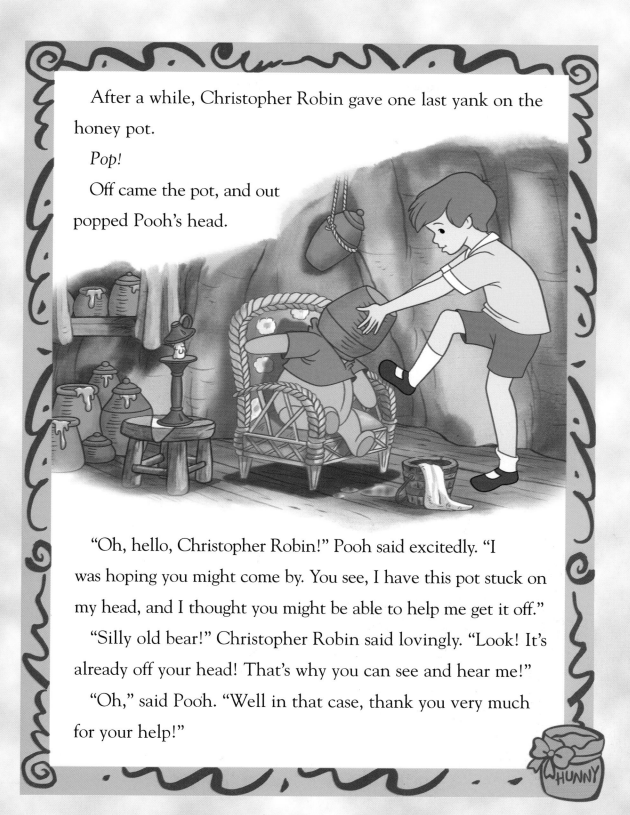

"Oh, hello, Christopher Robin!" Pooh said excitedly. "I was hoping you might come by. You see, I have this pot stuck on my head, and I thought you might be able to help me get it off."

"Silly old bear!" Christopher Robin said lovingly. "Look! It's already off your head! That's why you can see and hear me!"

"Oh," said Pooh. "Well in that case, thank you very much for your help!"

Feeling very grateful for his friend's kindness, Pooh asked Christopher Robin to stay for supper. Christopher Robin gladly accepted, and the two good friends had a wonderful evening.

"Oh, Christopher Robin, I'm so glad you stopped by," Pooh said.

"Me, too, Pooh," Christopher Robin said.

Later on, Pooh began to look at the bottom
of his honey pot to finish off the very last
smackerel of his delicious supper.
But this time, Christopher Robin
made sure that Pooh used his
paw instead of his head
to get it!

Disney
DONALD DUCK

Peace and Quiet, Please

"**W**ak!" Donald cried, tumbling out of his hammock.

"Stop—you no-good cattle rustlers!" Huey yelled, as he galloped by on a stick hobbyhorse.

"Ha-ha!" laughed Dewey, leaping over Donald.

"Ha-ha!" laughed Louie, right behind his brother. "Sheriff Huey can't catch us!" he shouted.

"Yow—ow!" Donald sputtered. The ends of Dewey's and Louie's hobbyhorses jabbed and poked him.

His nephews stopped playing. "Thanks for these great hobbyhorses, Unca Donald," his nephews said.

"Wanna play?" Huey asked.

"No, thanks. This is my weekend off. My two days to do whatever I please. And all I want is to have a little peace and quiet, *please*!" Donald said.

"Okay. Bye, Unca Donald!" the nephews called.

"Hmmmf," snorted Donald.

Donald tried to untangle the hammock, but he only succeeded in tying it into knots.

"Well," thought Donald, giving up on untangling the hammock. "I really didn't want to take a nap now, anyway. And I did tell the boys to have fun. Maybe I'll work on my ship model of *Miss-Daisy*-in-a-bottle, instead."

Donald went into his den and took down the fragile ship-in-a-bottle that he had been building for months. He carefully unwrapped the parts that still needed to be glued onto the ship and picked up a delicate mast. Donald slowly slipped his hand into the bottle. He almost had the mast in position when suddenly the floor began to shake.

"Now get ready, girls. And a 5-6-7-8 . . . ," Daisy shouted above the pounding music.

"Hmmmf," moaned Donald when the mast snapped in half. He had forgotten that Daisy's All-Girl Tap and Drum Corps were practising in the playroom that morning.

"The regional All-Girl Tap and Drum Corps performance is at the old theatre tonight," Donald said to himself. "So they need to practise. Too bad the new theatre isn't finished. If it were, Daisy and her team would be practising there. Instead, here they are tapping and drumming and shaking *my* house."

There was no way Donald could work on *Miss Daisy* while Daisy and her friends were dancing. Frustrated, Donald packed a sandwich, grabbed his fishing rod, and headed out the door.

"Ah, peace and quiet at last!" Donald sighed, after rowing to his best fishing spot. With his line baited and his rod in one hand, Donald unwrapped his sandwich to begin to eat. But before he could take a bite, waves rocked the boat and threw Donald against the side.

Vrooom! Vrooom! roared a high-speed motorboat. "Hi ya, Donald!" hollered Goofy on water skis.

"I didn't know Goofy could water ski," thought Donald. "Uh-oh!" he shouted.

Goofy was coming closer and closer and faster and faster and was heading right towards Donald's little rowing boat. Donald held on to the sides of the boat. The wake from the motorboat tossed the little rowing boat back and forth as if it were a toy.

"Don't wave, Goofy!" Donald thought. "Don't let go of the rope."

"Hi ya, Donald!" Goofy hollered again *and* waved. "Oh no!" cried Donald.

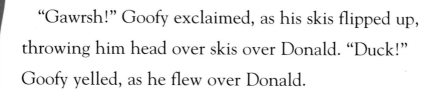

"Gawrsh!" Goofy exclaimed, as his skis flipped up, throwing him head over skis over Donald. "Duck!" Goofy yelled, as he flew over Donald.

And duck Donald did—just in time. "Hmmmf!" snorted a soggy Donald Duck, dripping from head to foot.

"Sorry, Donald! See ya later!" Goofy shouted, skiing away.

"Well, he's having a good time," muttered Donald. "Maybe I still can, too," Donald said, reeling in his fishing line.

"What's this?" Donald wondered, feeling a slight tug on his line. Carefully, he reeled in and lifted the line out of the water. It was a fish! A shimmering, golden fish! Donald had never seen anything like it. He gently took the hook out of the fish's mouth and put the creature in a pail of water.

The fish looked at Donald and winked. "Release me, fisherman, for I am magic and can make your wishes come true."

Donald shook his head in disbelief, "Ha—a magic fish?" he scoffed. "I don't believe it—

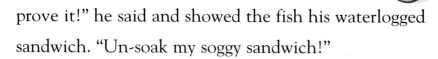

prove it!" he said and showed the fish his waterlogged sandwich. "Un-soak my soggy sandwich!"

"I can do better than that," the fish promised. Then she shivered and shook her golden scales. In a magical flash, an enormous picnic basket filled with Donald's preferred foods appeared.

"Wak! I'm convinced!" exclaimed Donald, putting the fish back in the lake.

But before she swam away, the magical fish said, "You have two more wishes, fisherman. Whatever you wish for, I will grant. Use the wishes wisely and well."

"Oh, boy!" Donald cried, diving into the picnic basket. As he ate, he thought about all the things he might wish for. "I could wish for *Miss-Daisy*-in-a-bottle to be finished or some much-needed peace and quiet. Or, maybe I should think bigger and wish for as much money as Uncle Scrooge has. Then I can pay for the theatre to be built faster for Miss Daisy."

Little did Donald know, it wouldn't be that simple. . . .

Donald quickly rowed back to shore, tied up his boat, and ran home. Racing up the steps, he tripped over a hobbyhorse. "Wak!" exclaimed Donald, as Huey, Dewey, and Louie ran in and tripped over their uncle.

"Sorry, Unca Donald," they cried.

"I wish we had real horses," Dewey added, helping his uncle stand up. "Maybe we wouldn't be tripping over you all the time."

"Oh yeah," cried Huey and Louie.

Not thinking, Donald said, "I wish you could, too."

Instantly there was a magical flash, and Huey, Dewey, and Louie were riding real horses.

"Thanks, Unca Donald!" they shouted, riding away.

"Hmmmf," Donald thought. "They're happy. . . ."

Donald went back inside to find his piggy bank. But instead, he found a note from Daisy. It read:

> *Donald Dear, thank you for letting us practise in*
> *the playroom. We went to the old theatre for*
> *a final dress rehearsal before tonight. See you*
> *then! Love, Daisy.*

Just as Donald finished reading the note, he heard *Brrrrng—Brrrrng! Brrrrng—Brrrrng!* It was the fire alarm, calling all of the volunteer firefighters to a fire.

From his house, Donald could see the building that was on fire. It was the old theatre—the same old theatre where Daisy and the All-Girl Tap and Drum Corps were performing that evening. It was the same old theatre where Daisy and her team had gone for a dress rehearsal!

"Oh no!" wailed Donald, as he grabbed his firefighter's gear and dashed out of the house.

The firefighters soon had the blaze under control. But the old theatre was beyond saving, and the new theatre was only half-finished.

Daisy ran to Donald, sobbing. He put his arm around her. "Oh," Daisy cried, "I wish the new theatre were ready!"

"I do, too," Donald said in sympathy. In a flash the new theatre was magically built. Daisy's tears dried immediately.

Daisy hugged Donald and said, "Now we can have our show tonight! And we can have our dress rehearsal right on time." Surprised and thrilled, she and her All-Girl Tap and Drum Corps rushed into the new theatre.

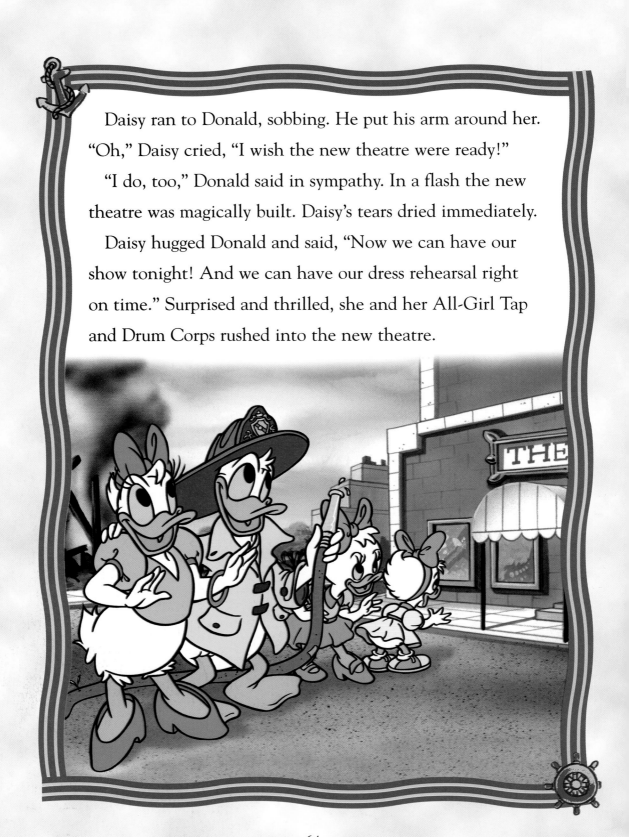

"Hmmmf—they're happy," said Donald, as he wandered back to his yard. "What an afternoon! All I wanted was a little peace and quiet. And what happens? Magic fish, horses for my nephews, a new theatre for Daisy—and a small feast for me," Donald said, sighing.

As Donald sat down in his hammock, he realized Huey, Dewey, and Louie had untangled it. "Wow! Looks like I got my peace and quiet after all," a contented Donald said, "and family and friends who are happy, too. Hmmmf—not bad for a single day."

Quasimodo–
The Kid Sitter

"Quasimodo, would you take care of Djali for me today?" Esmeralda asked one morning. "Phoebus and I have to go out."

"Djali and I could come with you," Quasimodo offered, looking up from a figure he was carving. "It would be fun."

"We need to run this errand alone," answered Esmeralda. "Please help me. I'll leave some hay for Djali to eat. I'm sure he won't be any trouble."

"All right," Quasimodo agreed, a bit disappointed.

Djali didn't want to be left behind, either. So when Esmeralda started to leave, he grabbed her skirt in his mouth and tugged.

"Now Djali—behave," said Esmeralda. She freed her skirt and left.

Djali was angry. He kicked his heels against the door and bleated. He ran outside onto the parapet and butted his head against the stone gargoyles, which were Quasimodo's friends. Then Djali ran off again.

"Quasimodo, this kid needs discipline," Hugo and Victor complained.

"Let me at him. I'll cool his heels," said Laverne.

"I'm sorry," Quasimodo apologized. "I'll take him into my workroom so that he won't bother you again."

Quasimodo led Djali into the workroom. "Please behave, Djali," pleaded Quasimodo.

"*Baah, baah, baah,*" Djali answered sadly.

"I know you wanted to go with Esmeralda and Phoebus," Quasimodo answered. "So did I. But we can have a nice time together. Wait here, and I'll bring you some hay to eat." And Quasimodo hurried off to get the hay.

While he was gone, Djali looked around the workroom. It was filled with interesting things that Quasimodo had made. Sitting on a long wooden table were tiny figures and houses that Quasimodo had carved and painted. Djali didn't know what they were. But they looked very tasty.

Crunch! Djali chomped on a figure of a man in a yellow hat. *Chomp!* He chewed a plump lady in a green gown. *Blecch!* The tiny figures looked better than they tasted.

Then Djali noticed a beautiful mobile hanging above the table. It was made of many bits of glass that sparkled in the light coming through the window. The deep purple and bright red glass pieces reminded Djali of grapes and apples— the fruits he loved best!

With a happy bleat, Djali leapt onto the table. He stood on his hind legs and pawed at the mobile with his forelegs, making it swing close enough to grab with his mouth.

Just then Quasimodo returned with his arms full of hay. "Djali, what are you doing?" exclaimed Quasimodo. "Get down right now!"

Startled, Djali turned and jumped, but his forelegs became tangled in the mobile strings. *Crash!* Djali fell to the floor, pulling the mobile down with him. Tangled in the mobile strings, Djali skittered and scampered around the room, knocking bits of glass, hay, and wooden figures everywhere.

"*Baah, baah,*" Djali bleated. Finally, Quasimodo caught Djali and untangled him.

"Djali, what am I going to do with you?" Quasimodo asked and sighed. "I have to clean up this mess. But I'm afraid you'll get into more trouble and get hurt even more while I work."

Finally, Quasimodo had an idea. He found a long piece of rope and tied it to Djali's collar. He led the little goat out onto the parapet and tied the other end of the rope to Laverne. Then Quasimodo put down a pile of hay for Djali to eat.

"Get that goat away from me," Laverne hissed at Quasimodo.

Djali thought he heard something. He looked around quickly. But Laverne snapped her mouth shut just in time.

"It's only for a few minutes, Laverne," answered Quasimodo. "I'll be right back."

With a puzzled frown, Djali glanced around to see whom Quasimodo was talking to. He stared at Laverne suspiciously.

Laverne stared back and held still. Djali blinked, shook his head, and began to eat his hay.

As soon as Djali wasn't looking, Laverne slipped the rope off and gave him a swift little push. Startled, Djali jumped away. Then, with a happy bleat, he realized that the rope was loose! He was free!

Skipping and jumping, Djali ran around and around the parapet. Then he climbed on Laverne's head and leapt up onto the edge of the cathedral roof. Climbing looked like fun. So up Djali went.

Just as Djali started to climb, Quasimodo came out. "I'm sorry I—," Quasimodo said, stopping short and looking around. Djali was nowhere to be seen!

"Djali—Djali, where are you?" called Quasimodo. He rushed to the edge of the parapet and looked down. He was frightened. What if Djali had fallen?

Then Quasimodo heard a mischievous bleat from the rooftop. There was Djali, peeking around a spire.

"Djali, come down!" Quasimodo shouted. "You'll fall!"

But Djali just bleated and climbed higher.

Quasimodo started to climb after the little goat. Up and up, higher and higher he went. But each time he got close to Djali, the little goat scampered out of reach.

At last, Djali climbed to the very top of the cathedral. Now there was nowhere else for him to go.

Then Djali looked down. The ground was very far away. A strong wind was blowing around the spires and towers. It felt to Djali as if the wind wanted to push him off the cathedral. Suddenly climbing wasn't fun anymore. He was afraid.

"Djali, come back down," pleaded Quasimodo. But Djali was too frightened to move. His feet felt frozen in place. All he could do was stand still and cry.

Quasimodo finally reached him. "It's all right, Djali," Quasimodo comforted. "I'm here to help you." He lifted the frightened goat onto his shoulders and began to climb down.

From far below, Quasimodo heard someone calling his name. He looked down and saw Esmeralda and Phoebus racing up the cathedral steps. Just then Quasimodo's foot slipped.

With a loud cry, he and Djali slid down the roof and tumbled over the parapet.

"Help!" shouted Quasimodo, as he and Djali flew past the gargoyles. Laverne saw the end of Djali's rope go slithering past her base. Instantly she grabbed it, jumped on it, and then froze in place before anyone could see her move.

With a jerk, the rope tightened and held. For a second Djali and Quasimodo dangled in the air. Quasimodo quickly reached up and grabbed the rope just above Djali. Hanging by one hand, he lifted Djali back onto his shoulders. Then hand over hand, Quasimodo pulled himself and Djali up the rope to the parapet.

Esmeralda and Phoebus were waiting to pull Quasimodo and Djali to safety. For a long time, the friends laughed and cried and hugged each other without speaking.

At last, Esmeralda wiped her eyes. "Oh, dear!" she exclaimed. "I was so upset that I almost forgot. Come down to the street, Quasimodo. Phoebus and I have a surprise for you and Djali."

Standing in the town square was a beautiful little wooden cart. While Quasimodo gazed at the cart, Esmeralda slipped a red leather harness with bells over Djali's head. "Don't you look handsome, Djali," she said.

"Our errand today was to get this cart for you," explained Esmeralda. "That's why I asked you to take care of Djali. We wanted the cart and harness to be a surprise for you both. Now you can go for rides in the country with us. And Djali will pull you whenever you need."

"I hope this cart makes up for all the trouble Djali caused you today," Esmeralda continued quietly.

For a moment Quasimodo was too surprised and delighted to answer. He simply watched Djali dancing happily along to the jingle of his harness bells.

"Friends do things for each other," Quasimodo answered, smiling. "You needed me to watch Djali and so I did. Just as you two knew I needed a cart and Djali needed a new harness and would love some bells."

Walt Disney's
Sleeping Beauty

Briar Rose
To the Rescue

Briar Rose awoke with a sleepy yawn and stretched. She looked out the window of her little room in the cottage. It looked like spring—how delightful!

After she had dressed, Briar Rose went to the kitchen to greet her three aunts—Flora, Fauna, and Merryweather.

"Good morning, dear!" called Flora.

"It's the first day of spring!" Fauna said.

"You slept late again," grumbled Merryweather. But she thoughtfully placed a biscuit with extra honey at Briar Rose's place at the table.

Briar Rose smiled. Merryweather liked to sound grumpy, but Briar Rose knew her aunt loved her.

"I suppose we have to do our spring cleaning today," Merryweather added.

"Yes, dear," replied Fauna. "That's what we always do on the first day of spring."

"I'm afraid we're going to need a new broom," Flora said. "This old one is quite ragged and dirty from all of our winter cleaning."

"Why don't I make a new broom?" Briar Rose offered. "I'll go out and find some straw and a nice sturdy, straight stick."

"Why, that's very sweet of you!" said Flora.

"Dress warmly, my dear," added Fauna. "It's still cold out, you know."

"Don't stay out long," Merryweather said. "You'll leave all the work for us!"

Briar Rose tried hard not to smile. She knew that
Merryweather wasn't worried about the work. She was
worried about Briar Rose's safety.

Briar Rose wrapped her cloak around herself, picked up her
basket, and stepped out the door.

"Don't try to walk on the ice!" Merryweather shouted after
Briar Rose. "It can break easily, now that it's melting."

Of course, Briar Rose already knew how dangerous the woods could be in springtime. Big chunks of snow could fall from trees, and dangerously thin ice could cover the pond.

In the shed, Briar Rose gathered straw for the new broom. As she put the straw into the basket, two little chipmunks appeared and began to chatter at her.

"Well, come on, then," invited Briar Rose. The chipmunks happily jumped into her basket.

Then some cheery bluebirds chirped at her from some rafters in the shed.

"You can come, too," said Briar Rose.

Other birds and animals
joined them. Soon all the friends
were parading happily through the woods.

As they approached the pond, Briar Rose noticed a flutter of
activity. She stopped singing and started worrying just a little.
What could be causing such a commotion?

The bluebirds flew ahead to see what was happening.
Briar Rose raced after them, with Merryweather's warning
echoing in her head: *Don't try to walk on the ice! It can break
easily, now that it's melting.*

Sure enough, Merryweather had been right. As Briar Rose reached the pond, the chipmunks started chattering and fidgeting to get out of the basket. When Briar Rose set down the basket, the chipmunks quickly jumped out and joined a group of animals gathered around the pond. All the animals were very upset as they watched a deer that had fallen through the ice.

Even though the deer was just a few feet from shore, the poor thing was struggling on the slippery ice to pull itself out to safety.

After watching for a few minutes, Briar Rose knew there was no way that the deer was going to get out on its own.

Briar Rose knew this deer well. It was a doe, and she was going to give birth very soon. Briar Rose knew she had to help the doe—but how?

Thinking quickly, Briar Rose hurried over to a nearby fallen tree. She broke off a long, sturdy branch and stretched it towards the deer. The deer tried to reach the branch but was so panicked that she was losing her strength. Growing increasingly concerned, Briar Rose wondered what she could do to calm the deer.

Suddenly Briar Rose had an idea. She began to sing the softest, most soothing lullaby she knew. Soon the doe started to calm down. Then the tired creature was able to grab the branch in her mouth.

Briar Rose carefully tugged and pulled until at last the doe was able to climb up onto the bank of the pond. Briar Rose sighed with relief—until she realized how hard the deer was shaking!

"Oh, you poor thing!" cried Briar Rose. "You're half-frozen!" She pulled a big handful of straw from her basket and began to rub it briskly over the deer's body. The doe's coat was beginning to dry, but she was still shivering.

"Come on, everyone!" Briar Rose said. She and the other animals led the deer through the woods.

When they finally reached her aunts' cottage, Briar Rose and the animals burst through the front door. She led the doe directly to the warm fireplace, leaving a trail of muddy hoofprints all over the floor.

"Oh, my!" cried Flora, when the aunts came into the room.

"We'll have to clean all over again," Fauna said.

"Oh, phooey!" said Merryweather. "Who cares about all that? How can we help, Briar Rose?"

"She fell through the—," Briar Rose started to say.

"Humph! I told you something like that would happen," Merryweather interrupted.

"We need to get her warm—," continued Briar Rose.

"And dry and fed!" again Merryweather interrupted. "Now step to it, ladies!"

Flora, Fauna, Merryweather, and Briar Rose worked together to make the deer comfortable. They dried the mother-to-be and made her a warm bed in the hay, lined with soft blankets. Then they gave the doe plenty of food and water. The deer soon fell asleep and slept through the night and most of the following day.

Briar Rose moved the doe to the shed that evening. Little by little, the doe came to trust Briar Rose, Flora, Fauna, and Merryweather. A little later that spring, the doe gave birth to not one, but two beautiful fawns.

Every morning, Briar Rose would go to the shed to begin her chores. She always noticed that someone had been there before her. And that person had been bringing the doe and fawns special treats. Can you guess who it was?

It was Merryweather, of course.